P9-BZR-352

Let's Have
a Play

Modern Curriculum Press
BEGINNING
TO
READ
Series

Let's Have a Play

Margaret Hillert

Illustrated by Sharon Elzaurdia

ISBN: 0-8136-5594-3
Printed in the United States of America

    22 23 24 25 26   06 05 04

Modern
Curriculum
Press

Pearson Learning Group

1-800-321-3106
www.pearsonlearning.com

Look at this.
What a day!
What can we do?
What is there for
us to do?

Here is something to play with.
Come here, girl.
What a good girl you are.
We like you.

Now we can look at books.
It is fun to do that.
It is fun to read.

Oh, look here.

Look at this.

Here is something to do.

We can make something.

We can have a play.

Here is how to do it.

See.
Here is how to do it.
Look at this and this.

Get to work.
Work, work, work.
We have to have this
for the play.

Now we have to make
a boy and a girl.
But how do we do that?
Oh, I see.

Father, Father.
Do you have what we want?
Look here.
Here is what we want.

Yes, I have something.
Is this it?
Will it work?

We will see.
We will work at it.
We will make something good.

Make something like this.

Make one.

Make two.

Now make one like this.
It will go here.

And make something red.
We have to have this.

And look what comes out.
It is funny.

Oh, oh.
Do not forget something
here and here.

And now make something for
up here.

Good. Good.
I have a boy.
You have a girl.

Here is a dog, too.
Look here.
This is a pretty good dog.

And here is something.
Look at this.
Do you like it?
What fun this is!

Oh, this looks good now.
We will have fun with it.
Let's get Mother and Father.
Run, run.

Mother. Father.
Come see what we did.
Oh, it is good.
You will see.
Sit down. Sit down.

Yes, it is good.
You did good work.
We like it.
Now, let's see the play

30

Margaret Hillert, author and poet, has written many books for young readers. She is a former first-grade teacher and lives in Birmingham, Michigan.

Let's Have a Play uses the 64 words listed below.

a	get	oh	us
and	girl	one	up
are	go	out	
at	good		we
		play	want
books	have	pretty	what
boy	here		will
but	how	read	with
		red	work
can	I	run	
come(s)	is		yes
	it	see	you
day		sit	
did	let's	something	
do	like		
dog	look(s)	that	
down		the	
	make	this	
Father	Mother	there	
for		to	
forget	not	too	
fun	now	two	
funny			